BIRDBRAIN AMOS

Written and illustrated by

MICHAEL DELANEY

PUFFIN BOOKS

In chapter three, Amos tells Kumba he can't tell her how happy he is. Well, there are two people I can't tell how happy I am—or thank enough—that this story has been published. One is my agent, Wendy Schmalz, who was determined to find *Birdbrain Amos* a home. The other is my editor with Philomel Books, Michael Green, who provided that home (as well as some excellent editorial advice).

Resemblance to any hippopotamus, tick bird, or other animal, wild or in captivity, is purely coincidental.

PUFFIN BOOKS
Published by Penguin Group
Penguin Young Readers Group,
345 Hudson Street, New York, New York 10014, U.S.A.
Penguin Books Ltd, 80 Strand, London WC2R ORL, England
Penguin Books Australia Ltd, 250 Camberwell Road, Camberwell, Victoria 3124, Australia
Penguin Books Canada Ltd, 10 Alcorn Avenue, Toronto, Ontario, Canada M4V 3B2
Penguin Books (N.Z.) Ltd, 182-190 Wairau Road, Auckland 10, New Zealand

First published in the United States of America by Philomel Books,
a division of Penguin Putnam Books for Young Readers, 2002
Published by Puffin Books, a division of Penguin Young Readers Group, 2004

1 3 5 7 9 10 8 6 4 2

The text is set in Cooper Old Style Light.
The art for this book was created with pen and ink on watercolor paper.

THE LIBRARY OF CONGRESS HAS CATALOGED THE PHILOMEL BOOKS EDITION AS FOLLOWS:
Delaney, M.C. (Michael Clark)
Birdbrain Amos / written and illustrated by Michael Delaney.
p. cm.
Summary: When Amos the hippopotamus advertises for a bird to help him with his bug problem, the tick bird
who answers his ad creates a different set of problems for him by building a nest on Amos's head.
ISBN: 0-399-23614-7 (hc)
[1. Hippopotamus—Fiction. 2. Cattle egret—Fiction.]
I. Title.
PZ7.D37319 Bi 2002 [Fic]—dc21 00-066932
Puffin Books ISBN 0-14-240031-9
Printed in the United States of America

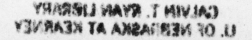

For Emma

Contents

Chapter One
HELP WANTED

Amos thought he would go crazy. Bugs and ticks were crawling all over his body, and being a hippopotamus, he had *quite* an enormous body. Insects were biting him on his head, back, belly, and legs. None of the other hippopotamuses who lived along the wide, lazy-flowing river seemed troubled by bugs. But then, they all had little birds who ate the bugs off their bodies. Amos decided that he, too, needed to find himself a little bird—and fast.

But where? Amos asked his friend Zamu how he found his bird.

"I advertised," said Zamu.

"You did?" said Amos, marveling at his friend's cleverness.

So that's what Amos did. He had some baboons broadcast an advertisement. Here is what Amos had them say:

> **Help wanted.** Bird needed to remove bugs from hippopotamus. Excellent pay and benefits. Experience a must. **Contact Amos.**

From way up high in the jungle treetops, the baboons yelled out Amos's message. Down on the ground, Amos listened. He was so proud. He had thought long and hard about his advertisement, selecting just the right words, phrasing them just so. Unfortunately, he forgot one detail. It was a small omission, a mere word. He neglected to say *what* kind of bird he was looking for.

The first bird to respond to Amos's advertisement was an African thrush.

"I'm interested in the bird position," said the thrush. The little bird was perched on a leafy vine that looped down from a moss-covered tree.

"Tell me about yourself," said Amos. He made himself comfortable in the muck and lily pads.

"I can sing Bach," boasted the thrush. He burst into a Bach cantata.

"That's wonderful," said Amos. "But can you—"

"Sing Beethoven?" asked the thrush. "You bet I can!" He launched into a rousing rendition of Beethoven's Ninth Symphony.

"That's very good," said Amos. He felt a bug creeping up his neck and tried to slap it with his hoof. "But can you—"

"Sing the Beatles?" asked the thrush. "Absolutely!" Tossing his head from side to side, the thrush whistled a jumpy version of "She Loves You."

Before he could be interrupted again, Amos blurted, "Yes, but can you remove bugs?"

The thrush stopped whistling and focused

his eyes on Amos. "Exactly how many bugs are we talking about?" he asked.

Amos shrugged. "I've never counted."

"Well, to be perfectly honest," said the thrush, "I'd much rather sing than remove bugs."

"But I don't need music in my life right now," said Amos. "I need a bird to remove these infernal bugs."

"But my singing will make you forget all about bugs," promised the thrush. "I know more than just the three B's—Bach, Beethoven, Beatles—if that's what you are concerned about. I know Stravinsky, Tchaikovsky, Copland, Ives, Sinatra, Louie Armstrong. I even know show tunes." The thrush began whistling "Oklahoma."

"Don't get me wrong," said Amos. "I'm very impressed with your singing ability. But

5

I'm afraid I need a bird with a bit more experience at removing bugs. Thank you for inquiring about my ad, though."

The thrush flew off—and not a moment too soon for Amos. "I'd go crackers if I had to listen to that singing all day long," he thought.

Chapter Two
THE VULTURE

The next bird to call on Amos was a vulture.

"I haven't actually removed bugs from animals," said the vulture. "But I have removed flesh from animal bones."

Amos cringed. "That's disgusting!" he said.

The vulture threw back her long bony neck and laughed.

It was a shrill, chilling laugh. It sent shivers down Amos's spine.

"I can understand why bugs would love to bite you," she said. "I'm sure you're a very tasty fellow. All that delicious meat. Mmm, I bet you taste scrumptious." The vulture smacked her beak.

Amos shuddered. "Well, thank you for answering my advertisement," he said. "I'll be in touch if I decide to hire you. No need to call me if you don't hear anything."

"Let me show you what I am capable of," said the vulture, and she hopped onto Amos's back.

Amos shrieked in horror. "*Ahhhhh!*" He plunged into the deepest part of the river. With a loud squawk, the vulture flew away.

Amos was trembling from head to hoof

when he surfaced on the river. The other hippopotamuses roared with laughter.

"You ninny, Amos!" said Zamu. "Don't you know anything? You can't have just any bird remove bugs from your body. You need a *tick* bird."

Amos's large gray face reddened. He was so embarrassed.

"Excuse me," a small female voice spoke up from the muddy riverbank. Amos turned and saw a slate-brown bird with a reddish-orange beak. "Could you direct me to Amos?"

"I'm Amos," sighed the hippopotamus.

"I'm a tick bird and I'd like to apply for the—"

"*You're* a tick bird?" cried Amos excitedly. "You're hired!"

"I don't do teeth," said the tick bird.

"Fine!" said Amos. "When can you start?"

"Immediately," replied the tick bird. And with that she flew up and snatched a bug that was crawling on Amos's face, right between his eyes. She swallowed the bug whole. Then she hopped onto the top of Amos's head and gobbled up another bug that was by his ear.

It felt wonderful. Relaxing, Amos closed

his eyes and said, "By the way, what's your name?"

"Kumba," responded the tick bird as she raced down Amos's spine, eating up every bug in sight.

"*Ooh,* Kumba!" said Amos with a chuckle. "That tickles!"

Chapter Three
KUMBA

The next few days were heaven for Amos. Kumba proved to be a regular dynamo at removing ticks and bugs. A hard worker, eager and motivated, she was everything an employer could ask for. Goodness knows, she had more than enough insects to keep her busy. As Amos stood in the river, he found that if he peered at his reflection in the water, he could see Kumba's reflection, too. She scrambled about his body, gulping down bug after bug after bug.

"I can't tell you how happy I am with you, Kumba," said Amos.

Kumba came up over the top of Amos's head and stopped. She looked startled. "You're not happy?" she said.

"No, I am," said Amos.

"You just said you can't tell me how happy you are."

"I can't," replied Amos.

"Well, then, why can't you tell me?"

"I did tell you," said Amos.

"You did?"

"I thought I did," said Amos, growing more and more confused. He decided to change the subject. "You must be exhausted," he said. "Please, relax! Make yourself at home."

"Here?" said Kumba.

"Wherever you like," said Amos.

"I like it here."

"Then make yourself at home there."

Kumba sat down on top of Amos's head, between his ears. She peered about and said, "I never realized what a nice view you have from up here."

Amos laughed. "I'm not surprised," he said. "You never stop long enough to look."

"I've stopped now," said Kumba.

"That's because I told you to," said Amos. "You work so hard, Kumba, I get tired just from watching you."

"I'm sorry if I make you tired," said Kumba.

"You don't really make me tired, Kumba."

"But you said I make you tired."

"It was just a joke," said Amos.

"That was a joke?" asked Kumba.

"Yes, a joke," Amos said.

"I didn't realize it was a joke," said Kumba.

"It was," said Amos.

Kumba certainly knew how to ruin a perfectly good joke. Amos decided not to tell Kumba any more jokes.

Suddenly, Kumba flew off. Sighing, Amos trudged, dripping wet, onto the muddy shore. He walked into a marsh of tall green reeds. He was the only hippopotamus in the reeds at that time of day. Hippopotamuses, who are vegetarians, tend to eat at night, and sleep or lie idly about during the day.

While Amos was chomping away on some reeds, he saw Kumba return to his head with a long reed in her beak. Amos thought nothing of it. But when Kumba flew off again and returned with a blade of grass, Amos began to wonder.

Being away from the river, Amos could

not glance at his reflection in the water and see what Kumba was up to. Kumba flew off again and again. Every time she returned, she had a reed or a twig or a piece of grass in her beak.

"Pardon me, Kumba," said Amos when the tick bird returned, this time with a twig in her beak. "But what, exactly, are you doing on top of my head?"

"I'm buuuling a est."

"I'm sorry," said Amos, "what did you say?"

"I'm buuuling a est."

"I can't understand a word you're saying."

Kumba set the twig down. "I'm building a nest."

Amos nearly choked on the reeds he was

chewing. "A *nest?*" he blurted, coughing, his eyes bulging. "You mean, a *bird*'s nest?"

"Yes, a bird's nest."

"*Why?*" asked Amos.

"Why what?" asked Kumba.

"Why are you building a bird's nest?"

"To lay eggs."

"On top of *my* head?"

"You told me to make myself at home."

"Yes, but I didn't mean . . ." Amos started to say when he realized that, once again, Kumba had misunderstood him.

Kumba asked, "You didn't mean what?"

Amos sighed. "To tell you the truth, Kumba, I don't know what I mean anymore."

Chapter Four
ZAMU

Amos had to lie down. What terrible luck to hire a tick bird who was about to lay eggs!

"Why *me*?" groaned Amos as he watched Kumba fly off to find more building material for her nest.

"*Psst, Amos,*" a voice whispered from the reeds.

Startled, Amos sprang to his feet. He whirled around and saw Zamu lying flat on his belly in the reeds. "Oh, hi, Zamu," said Amos.

"*Shhh!*" hushed Zamu. "I don't want any-one to see me with you."

"You don't?" asked Amos, surprised.

"What are you doing?" demanded Zamu.

"Eating reeds," replied Amos innocently.

"I mean, what are you doing with that ridiculous bird's nest on your head?"

"Oh, that," said Amos with a glance upward. "It wasn't my idea. I hired a tick bird the other day and she's building a nest."

"Well, I didn't think *you* were building it," said Zamu. "What are you going to do about it?"

"I don't know what I *can* do about it," said Amos.

"For goodness' sake, Amos, don't be a birdbrain! Take command of the situation!" exclaimed Zamu. "You're not going to let a timid little tick bird run your life, are you? Talk to her!"

"She's not that easy to talk to," said Amos. Then he asked, "What should I say to her?"

"Tell her she's fired!" said Zamu.

"That's kind of drastic, isn't it?" asked Amos.

"Wake up and smell the algae, Amos!" said Zamu. "You've become the laughing-stock of the river."

"I have?" said Amos, shocked. He glanced over at the river and saw a rhinoceros smirking at him. At least, it sure looked as if the rhinoceros was smirking. It was hard to tell,

though, with that big horn over the rhinoceros's mouth.

"You've got to get rid of her," said Zamu. "Your reputation is at stake."

"It is?" said Amos.

"Of course it is!" said Zamu. "Now get rid of her!" Keeping low to the ground, Zamu turned and slinked off into the reeds. Amos sighed. He knew Zamu was right. Zamu was always right.

But when Kumba flew back, Amos found he didn't have the heart to fire her just then. So he decided to put it off until the next morning.

"It really is a morning thing to do," he told himself.

Chapter Five
EGGS

Kumba, we need to talk," said Amos the next morning.

Kumba flew down from her nest. She lighted on a reed in front of Amos. "We do?" she said.

"Yes, we do," said Amos. "I thought I should tell you, Kumba, what hippopotamuses like and don't like. They like to lie about in the water and they like to stay out late at night and they like to eat plants and they like—"

"Do they like eggs?" interrupted Kumba.

"Eggs?" said Amos.

"Yes, eggs," said Kumba.

"Not to eat, they don't," said Amos.

"But if they don't eat them, do they like eggs?" asked Kumba.

Amos shrugged. "I guess they like eggs," he said. "I mean, they don't *dis*like them. But to get back to the point, Kumba, hippopotamuses like some things and don't like other things. One thing they don't like is—"

"Good thing they like eggs," said Kumba, "because I laid three this morning."

"Glad to hear it," said Amos. "Now, as I was saying, what hippopotamuses don't like is—did you say you laid eggs?"

"Three of them," replied Kumba.

"*Three eggs?*" cried Amos, aghast.

"Yes, three," said Kumba. "So, what don't hippopotamuses like?"

"Never mind," he sighed.

What was Amos to do? He couldn't fire Kumba now, not after she had laid her eggs. Yet, he couldn't possibly keep a nest with eggs on top of his head. What would the other hippopotamuses say? What would *Zamu* say?

"If only I had fired Kumba yesterday, like I was going to, I wouldn't be in this mess," thought Amos.

Chapter Six
THE PYTHON

Kumba returned to her nest. Amos, meanwhile, racked his brain, trying to figure out what to do about Kumba. By and by, Kumba came down from her nest.

"Could you do me a favor?" she asked.

"What kind of a favor?" asked Amos.

"A little favor," said Kumba.

"What kind of a little favor?" asked Amos.

"Could you keep an eye on my eggs?"

To be perfectly honest, this didn't sound to Amos like such a little favor. It sounded like a big favor. But he just said, "Why, where are you going?"

"I need a break," said Kumba.

"A break?" asked Amos.

"Yes, a break," said Kumba, arching her back. "I need to get out and fly around for a while. I've been sitting on my nest all day long."

Amos sighed. "Sure, I'll keep an eye on your eggs."

"Are you sure you don't mind?"

"Yes, I'm sure."

"Are you sure you're sure?"

"Yes, I'm sure I'm sure," said Amos. "Now go!"

Kumba flew off.

"Great," Amos grumbled. "Now I'm a baby-sitter."

"Tired of being taken advantage of?"

26

Amos heard a deep, understanding voice ask from above his head.

Startled, Amos peered up. A giant python was in a tree, dangling from a leafy branch.

"I sure am," said Amos.

"Feel like things are out of your control?"

"How did you know?" asked Amos.

The python smiled. "Good news, my friend. Your troubles are over."

"They are?" said Amos in surprise.

The python nodded. "I have a guaranteed method that gets rid of tick birds fast."

"You do?" said Amos.

"What's more, there's no unsightly mess. No annoying feathers to clean up."

"It sounds great," said Amos.

"It *is* great," agreed the python. "But that's not all. I can also get rid of pesky rodents,

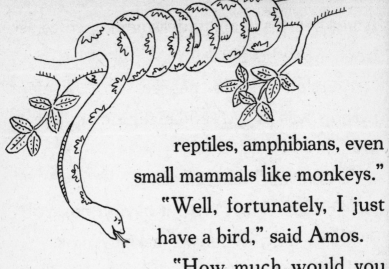

reptiles, amphibians, even small mammals like monkeys."

"Well, fortunately, I just have a bird," said Amos.

"How much would you expect to pay for my services?" asked the python.

"Gee, I don't know," said Amos.

"A small amount? A fair amount? A huge amount?"

Amos took a wild guess. "A huge amount," he said.

"If you act now," said the python, "I'll get rid of your tick bird for free."

"For *free*?" said Amos, amazed.

"That's right," said the python. "Absolutely free. It's a special limited time offer." The python stretched closer to Amos. "I see you also have some eggs on top of your head."

"Yes," groaned Amos.

"Tell you what," said the python. "I don't usually do this, but since you look like such a nice guy, I'll get rid of the eggs, too."

"You will?" said Amos.

"So what do you say?" asked the python. "Have we got a deal?"

"How can I say no?" said Amos.

The python smiled. "Good," he said.

"Exactly how do you intend to get rid of Kumba?" asked Amos.

"Kumba?" asked the snake.

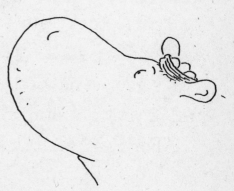

"The tick bird," said Amos.

"You leave the details to me," said the python.

With that, the snake dropped to the ground and slithered off, disappearing into the jungle.

Chapter Seven
CHA

Amos was perfectly delighted by this happy turn of events. "That sure is nice of that python to offer to help me," he thought.

Amos decided to find Zamu and tell him the good news. Just as he was about to start for the river, though, Kumba flew into view from around the river bend. She was with another tick bird. The two birds flew straight toward Amos.

"I'm so glad I ran into you," the other tick bird was saying. She was a small, plump bird with a big voice that carried far.

"I'm glad I ran into *you*," said Kumba.

"I'm glad you're glad," said the other tick bird.

"I'm glad you're glad that I'm glad," said Kumba.

"*This* is where you live?" said the other tick bird, amazed, as they glided down to Amos's head. "Why, Kumba, dear, it's *darling*."

Kumba landed on top of Amos's head. The other tick bird flew all about Amos, admiring Kumba's new home. Amos tilted his head back to get a better view of the tick bird.

Kumba let out a loud shriek: "*Eeeeeeeek!*"

She shrieked right into Amos's ears. Amos, cringing, shook his head.

"*Eeeeeeeeek!*" cried Kumba again.

"What is it?" asked the other tick bird.

"It's *him!*" said Kumba. "I'm sitting on a nest of fragile eggs and *he's* moving his head!"

"You let me handle this," said the other tick bird, taking charge.

The tick bird touched down in front of Amos. She glared at Amos as though he had committed a horrible crime. "What's your name?" she demanded.

She spoke in such a gruff manner, Amos didn't dare not tell her. "My name is Amos," he said.

"Well," said the tick bird. "I'm Cha. I'm a friend of Kumba's. Now pay close attention. I want you to hold your head up high."

The tick bird demonstrated how he

should stand. She threw back her shoulders, and thrust her head high. Amos did the same. Cha glanced over at Amos. Frowning, she shook her head.

"No! No! No!" she bellowed. "I said hold your head up *high!*"

Amos lifted his head higher.

"You call *that* holding your head up high?" asked Cha.

Amos strained to hold his head up even higher.

"Push those shoulders back!" barked Cha.

Amos pushed his shoulders back as far as he could push them.

"There, that's better!" exclaimed Cha. Now that Amos had it right, he stood as still as a statue. He did not move a muscle.

He glanced down at Cha. It was difficult to see her without moving his head.

"Egads, what's that crocodile got in his mouth?" cried Cha in horror.

Amos whirled about to take a look. The moment he did, Kumba cried, "*Eeeeeeek!*"

The next thing Amos knew, something sharp had stabbed him on the nose. It was Cha. She had flown up and pecked him with her beak!

"What's *that* for?" asked Amos.

"You moved your head!" replied Cha.

"I wanted to see the crocodile," said Amos.

"There was no crocodile," said Cha. "It was a test—and you failed! You moved your head!"

"A *test*?" exclaimed Amos. He couldn't

believe a tick bird was testing him. He was glad Zamu was not around to witness this.

Cha pointed her wing at a branch that was just above Amos's head. "Will you look at the size of that gorilla!" she cried.

Amos was all set to look up when he stopped. Keeping his head level, he lifted his eyes to the leafy branch that Cha had pointed to. There was no gorilla.

"*Excellent!*" said Cha. "*That's* how you keep your head straight."

Amos was pleased. "Now what happens?" he asked.

"Now you're going to stand perfectly still while I visit Kumba," said Cha, and flew up to the top of Amos's head.

Chapter Eight
A Terrible Misunderstanding

Kumba and Cha talked *forever*. They just chattered on and on. Amos thought Cha would never leave. At last, though, she said good-bye to Kumba. Then she flew down in front of Amos's face and said, "Now remember, Amos, stand up nice and tall."

"I'll remember," promised Amos.

Cha flew off. Amos, relieved, went to go look for Zamu again. He wandered up the lush riverbank, with Kumba atop his head. He was pushing through some rather tall reeds and vegetation when, from behind a bush, something sprang out at him.

It was the python!

The snake scared the daylights out of Amos. *"Aaaaahhhhh!"* he shrieked, leaping backward.

Kumba twittered loudly and flew off.

"You blithering idiot!" cried the python as he watched Kumba disappear behind the treetops across the river. "You scared the tick bird away."

"Well, I didn't know you were going to attack *me!*" said Amos, trembling.

"I wasn't attacking *you*," said the python crossly. "I was attacking the tick bird."

"You were?" said Amos. "Why?"

"I'm taking care of your tick bird problem," replied the python.

"*That's* your way of getting rid of Kumba?" asked Amos.

"How did you think I was going to get rid of her?" asked the python. "I'm a python. Pythons *eat* birds."

"Yes, I know, but—well, I didn't know—what I mean to say is—I'm afraid there's been a terrible misunderstanding!"

"Well, now that everything has been cleared up," said the snake, "would you kindly lower your head so I can gobble up those bird eggs."

"No!" said Amos, horrified. "I can't let you do that!"

"What do you mean you can't let me do that?" asked the python.

"I can't!" declared Amos.

"We had a deal, remember?" said the python.

"Yes, I know, but I didn't know that eating Kumba and her eggs was part of the deal."

"You're not breaking our deal, are you?" asked the python.

"I'm sorry," said Amos. "But I can't let you eat them. I hope you understand."

From the furious look in the python's eyes, it was clear he understood nothing.

"Very well," hissed the python as, twisting about, he slid away. "But mark my words: You haven't seen the last of me."

Chapter Nine
ANOTHER TICK BIRD

Alone, Amos groaned. "As if I don't have enough problems," he muttered. "Now I have a python mad at me."

Amos plopped down in a big splotch of sunlight that stretched across the riverbank. Closing his eyes, he tried to forget his troubles.

"Where's Kumba?" he heard a voice ask.

Amos opened his eyes. A new tick bird was standing before him.

"She flew off," replied Amos.

"When will she be back?" asked the tick
bird.

"She didn't say," said Amos, and closed
his eyes again.

"I didn't get it," said the tick bird.

Amos opened his eyes. "I beg your pardon?"

"I didn't get it," the tick bird said again.

"Didn't get what?"

"The job."

"What job?" asked Amos.

"The job I interviewed for," said the tick bird. "Didn't Kumba tell you?"

Amos shook his head. "I don't think so."

"I'm surprised she didn't tell you," said the tick bird. "I thought she would have told you."

"She didn't," said Amos.

"I wonder why she didn't tell you," said the tick bird.

"Maybe she forgot," offered Amos.

"She *forgot*?" cried the tick bird, looking terribly hurt. "How could she forget?"

"I said *maybe* she forgot," said Amos. "I didn't say for sure she forgot. It's quite possible Kumba told me, but I didn't realize she was telling me. If that's the case, it wouldn't be the first time we've misunderstood each other."

The tick bird nodded as though he understood. Then he said, "I really thought I had this job. I would've gotten to work for a hippopotamus."

"Is that so?" said Amos.

The tick bird nodded. "It's the story of my life," he said in a sad voice. "I go on one job interview after another, but I'm never offered a job. Hippos, rhinos, giraffes, elephants—they all say no." The tick bird gave Amos the most accusing stare. "Say, what is it with you big animals, anyway?"

"What do you mean?" asked Amos.

"I mean," said the tick bird, "I have so many outstanding qualities, you'd think I'd be hired on the spot. I'm handsome, witty, charming, entertaining, funny, delightful . . ."

The tick bird talked on and on about his many outstanding qualities. After a while,

Amos stopped listening. He stepped over to nibble on a clump of grass that was growing on the riverbank.

"You know," Amos heard the tick bird say, "the absolute best-tasting grass grows in the jungles along the western coast of India."

"I didn't know that," said Amos.

The tick bird nodded. "It's true," said the tick bird. "I once flew to India for a job interview."

"That's a long way to go for a job interview," said Amos.

"Oh, I've traveled all over," boasted the tick bird. "I've been to job interviews in Egypt, Kenya, South Africa, the Ivory Coast, the Philippines, Thailand, Malaysia . . . "

Chapter Ten
AKKA

The tick bird rattled off place after place. He was well on his way to naming every tropical country on earth, it seemed, when, luckily, Kumba returned. She flew down out of the sky and landed on the riverbank beside the tick bird.

"There you are!" said Kumba.

"There *you* are!" said the tick bird.

"I was wondering where you were," she said.

"I was wondering where *you* were," he said.

"You'll never guess what just happened," said Kumba.

"What just happened?" asked the tick bird.

"A snake tried to attack me!" said Kumba.

"A snake?" said the other tick bird, widening his eyes.

"A *big* snake!" said Kumba. "I shudder to think what would have happened if I hadn't flown away."

"I shudder, too," said the tick bird.

Kumba turned to Amos and said, "I see you've met my husband, Akka."

"This is your *husband*?" said Amos, surprised.

"I thought you'd met," said Kumba.

Amos shook his head. "I didn't say we'd met."

"I was under the impression you had met," said Kumba.

"I'm sorry if I gave you that impression," said Amos. "But I never said we met."

"But you have been talking to each other," said Kumba.

"Yes, we've been talking," said Amos.

"But you haven't met?"

"No, we haven't met."

"I'm confused," said Kumba.

"I'm confused, too," confessed Amos.

"I'm discouraged," said Akka. "I . . . I . . . I didn't get the job."

"Oh, you poor thing!" cried Kumba.

She went to comfort him. But Akka held up his wing to stop her. "Being the courageous bird that I am," he said, "I cannot allow myself to wallow in self-pity. Besides, I know someone who can help me find a job."

"Who?" asked Kumba.

"*Him!*" said Akka. He pointed his wing right at Amos.

"*Me?*" said Amos, surprised.

"Yes, *you!*" said Akka. "You're a hippopotamus. You know how hippopotamuses and other big animals think. You can tell me why none of you will hire me."

"What a great idea!" said Kumba.

"Isn't it?" said Akka. "You'd think a tick bird who comes up with such great ideas would have no trouble finding a job, wouldn't you?"

"You'd think," murmured Amos.

"So tell us, Amos. Why can't a clever bird like myself get a job?" asked Akka.

"Well . . . " said Amos, stalling.

He knew the answer, of course. A big animal doesn't want a courageous tick bird or a clever tick bird or even a charming tick bird. A big animal wants a tick bird who is good at getting rid of ticks and bugs. Amos didn't know quite how to tell Akka this, though. He didn't want to hurt the tick bird's feelings.

Amos took such a long time to answer that Akka finally said: "You need more time to think, don't you?"

"*Yes!*" cried Amos. "That's what I need! More time!"

Akka nodded understandingly. "You're like me," he said. "You can never think when you're put on the spot."

"I also need to be alone!" said Amos. "I always think

better when I'm by myself."

"I'm the exact same way," replied Akka. He turned to his wife, saying, "C'mon, dear. Amos needs time to think."

As the two birds flew off, Amos heard Akka say to Kumba: "Isn't it amazing that a hippopotamus and a tick bird could have so much in common!"

Chapter Eleven
MORE ADVICE

Holding his head high the way Cha had shown him, Amos rose and waded into the river. Keeping his head above the water, he swam about in the current. The other hippopotamuses gave Amos the fishiest looks. A few even smiled. Evidently, they thought it was some kind of gag—why else would a hippopotamus parade around proudly with a bird's nest on top of his head?

Wishing to avoid the other hippopotamuses—and their stares—Amos paddled into a lonely lagoon. He made himself comfortable among some lily pads. Closing his eyes, he was trying to forget his troubles when a very unexpected thing happened. Zamu popped up out of the lily pads right in front of Amos.

Startled, Amos opened his eyes wide. *"Zamu!"* he gasped. "Where'd you come from?"

"I thought you were going to fire that tick bird," said Zamu, shaking a lily pad off his head.

"I was going to," said Amos. "But she laid three eggs."

"So?" said Zamu.

"So I can't fire her now," said Amos. "It might disturb the eggs."

"They're not *your* eggs, are they?" asked Zamu.

"Well . . . no."

"Well, then," said Zamu. "What are you concerned about?"

"I'd hate to have something happen to the eggs," said Amos.

Zamu threw up his front hooves in frustration. For a moment, Amos thought Zamu was going to grab him and try to shake some sense into him. "Listen to me, you birdbrain," said Zamu. He stared straight into Amos's eyes. "Tick birds are *always* laying eggs. If anything happens to these eggs, she'll lay more. Trust me. Don't get involved!"

"But I already am involved," said Amos.

"Well, get yourself uninvolved!" Zamu told him.

Just then, from up the river, another hippopotamus floated into view. Zamu gasped. Zamu was so afraid to be seen with Amos, he vanished under the water. He was gone in the blink of an eye.

Alone, Amos heaved a huge sigh. He was annoyed at himself. Of course Zamu was right. "Why should I care what happens to the eggs?" he thought. "They're not *my* eggs! So what if they're disturbed and never hatch!"

But Amos knew that if that were ever to happen, he would never forgive himself.

Chapter Twelve
A Small Favor

Suddenly, over by the riverbank, a voice whispered, *"Amos!"*

Amos turned. Nobody was there.

"Over here!"

Cha stepped out from behind a large fern. "Where's Kumba?" she asked.

"She's out with her husband, Akka."

"That oaf!" muttered

Cha. Then she said, "I have a small favor to ask of you, Amos."

"You do?" said Amos.

Cha nodded. "Yes, I do. I need your help. I want to throw Kumba a surprise baby shower."

"Why do you need my help to do that?" asked Amos.

"I want to hold it on your back."

"*My back?*"

"I have it all figured out," said Cha. "You'll help me surprise her."

"Oh no, not me," said Amos. "I'm no good at surprises."

"Of course you are," said Cha. "So what do you say? Will you be part of our baby shower?"

"Well, I'd like to," said Amos, "except—"

"Except what?" said Cha with a fierce glare.

"Except, well, I um . . . "

"Yes?"

Amos could not think of a single good excuse. Or, at least, he could not think of one that would be good enough to satisfy Cha.

"Oh, all right," he said. "You can hold it on my back."

"Wonderful!" said Cha.

"How many tick birds are we talking about?" asked Amos. "Four or five?"

"Seventy-six," replied Cha.

"*Seventy-six!*" shouted Amos.

On the opposite shore, some zebras who were drinking from the river peered curiously up at Amos. Just above them, Kumba and Akka appeared in the sky.

"Now remember, Amos, mum's the word,"

said Cha. She hurriedly flew off into the jungle.

Akka and Kumba, wings outstretched, glided down, landing in front of Amos. "Any thoughts on why nobody will hire a charming tick bird like myself?" asked Akka.

"I'm still thinking," muttered Amos.

Akka turned to Kumba. "What did I tell you, Kumba?" he said. "I knew he wouldn't have an answer yet. Nor would I have! I tell you, Amos and I are like two peas in a pod."

Chapter Thirteen
SURPRISE!

On the day of the baby shower, Amos acted as if it was just an ordinary day. He slept late. He swam in the river. He lay about in the mud. He munched on some reeds. He slept some more. He did all these things because, quite frankly, he did not want to face the fact that he was part of a baby shower. He showed such a lack of enthusiasm, Kumba never suspected a thing was up.

In the late afternoon, Amos, as planned by Cha, wandered away from the river. While Kumba sat atop his head, Amos made his way through the reeds and tall grasses until he came to a clearing with an old gnarled umbrella tree. Beside the tree grew a big bush. At first glance, it looked as if not a soul was around. But if you peered long and hard enough at the bush, you would have noticed dozens upon dozens of little eyes peeking out.

"Kumba, could you please see if I have a bug on my back?" asked Amos—just as he had been instructed to by Cha.

Amos felt Kumba's little feet scurry down his back. "I don't see a bug," she said.

"Keep looking," said Amos.

Suddenly, from the bush, the tick birds rushed out of hiding.

"*SURPRISE!*" they screamed, flying straight at Kumba.

Kumba let out a startled shriek. She

clutched her wing to her breast and cried, "What's all this?"

"It's your baby shower!" announced Cha. She gave Kumba a big hug. Then she declared: "*Let's party!*"

And so the party began. The birds squeezed onto Amos's back. All seventy-six of them. They cheeped and twittered as they chatted to one another. They made such a loud racket, Amos was sure he would go deaf.

Akka, meanwhile, kept Amos company.

"This is my first baby shower," confessed Amos.

"Mine, too," said Akka.

Amos spied two tick birds flying his way.

They were carrying a big leaf between their beaks. The leaf was piled high with dead bugs.

"Who are those birds?" asked Amos.

"The caterers," replied Akka.

"The *caterers?*" cried Amos with bulging eyes.

Akka nodded. "Cha is having the party catered."

Amos noticed three African thrushes gliding down from the sky. "Who are they?" he inquired.

"That's the band," said Akka.

 "The *band?*" cried Amos. "Oh, and I suppose *that*'s the band leader," he said, glancing up at a pelican who was hovering above his head.

"No, that's the comedian," said Akka. "Cha thought it would be fun to have a comedian at the party. I tell you, Cha has thought of everything."

"So I see. . . . Any idea how long this thing will last?" grumbled Amos.

"Oh, about a week," replied Akka.

Amos gulped—but not because of what Akka had said. Less than a hundred yards away, who should emerge from the jungle

but Zamu! Head bowed, he was grazing on the high grasses.

Amos gasped, *"Oh, no!"*

Akka chuckled. "I'm only kidding, Amos," he said. "They don't really last a week."

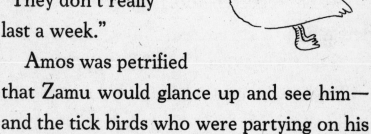

Amos was petrified that Zamu would glance up and see him— and the tick birds who were partying on his back. He panicked.

"That's it!" he said. "Party's over!"

"Hey, relax," said Akka, looking quite nervous. "I said I was only kidding."

Amos cried: "You tick birds heard what I said! The party is over! Now *scram!*"

The party screeched to a halt. Not a single bird so much as twittered. They looked terrified—all except Cha, that is. She looked annoyed. She flew down beside Akka.

"What's gotten into you, Amos?" she demanded.

"The party's over!" declared Amos.

To show he meant business, Amos vigorously shook his body. The birds darted into the sky. Even Cha and Akka flew away in fright.

Zamu heard the flapping of all the wings and glanced over.

"*Zamu!*" cried Amos, trying to sound, and look, amazed. He grinned. "What a delightful surprise to see you here! How's everything?"

Zamu eyed the nest on top of Amos's

head. He looked thoroughly disgusted. "I see you've still got that nest on top of your head."

"I do?" said Amos, startled, with a glance upward. "Well, what do you know, I guess I do!"

Chapter Fourteen
THE ELEPHANTS

Amos kept a low profile after the baby shower. That is, he kept as low a profile as a huge hippopotamus can keep. While Kumba sat upon her nest, Amos sat in the reeds and moped.

He hated himself for how he had acted at the baby shower. He hated that he hated himself for acting the way he did. Zamu would not have cared how he acted.

"Why can't I be more like Zamu?" Amos asked himself.

A small herd of elephants appeared on the opposite shore. The elephants had traveled a great distance. They looked hot and weary, and their enormous wrinkled gray bodies were powdered with dirt.

Amos sat quietly and watched the elephants refresh themselves in the cool

river. They slurped water into their trunks and hosed off their bodies.

By and by, Amos noticed that one of the elephants, a female, was eyeing him in a peculiar manner. It made Amos extremely uneasy.

"I love your hat!" the elephant called over.

Amos pretended not to hear.

"Is it your own creation?" she asked.

To Amos's surprise, another voice answered—a voice on top of his head.

"It's not a hat!" shouted Akka, who was visiting Kumba at the time. He wasn't annoyed at the elephant for confusing his wife's nest for a hat. He was merely clearing matters up. "It's a bird's nest!"

"A *bird's nest!*" the elephant echoed. "I've never seen a hippopotamus with a bird's nest on top of his head!"

The elephant trumpeted to the other elephants. "Hey, everybody, get a load of the hippo with a bird's nest on top of his head!"

"Oh, *great!*" muttered Amos.

The other elephants raced over to get a glimpse of Amos. "Will you look at *that!*" one of them marveled.

Amos thought he would scream.

"*Hey!*" cried Kumba all of a sudden.

"Hey what?" replied Amos, sulking.

"Hey, the eggs are hatching!" exclaimed Akka.

"They are?" cried Amos, leaping to his feet. "Are you sure?"

The answer came not from Kumba or Akka, but from the eggs themselves—that is, the baby birds. They began chirping loudly.

Chapter Fifteen
NAMES

Amos was so excited. At long last, he could fire Kumba. He could tell her to get lost—and take her family with her.

"Kumba," Amos called out. "Could I see you for a moment?"

To Amos's surprise, both Kumba and Akka landed in front of him.

"Now that your eggs have hatched," said Amos, fixing his gaze only upon Kumba, "it's time—"

Akka held up his wing and said, "We already know."

"You do?" said Amos, surprised.

Akka nodded. "You're going to say it's time you find out what Kumba had."

The truth was, the thought had never even entered Amos's mind. "What did she have?" he asked.

"Girls," said Akka. "We've decided to name one Kaza—"

"After my mother," said Kumba.

"We're naming another Nyayo—"

"After Akka's mother," said Kumba.

"And the third we're naming . . . "

"After *your* mother!" cried Kumba gleefully.

"*My* mother?" said Amos, stunned.

Akka chuckled. "You're just like me," he said. "I, too, would be shocked at a moment like this."

"But you don't even know my mother," said Amos.

"That's true," agreed Akka. "But we know *you*. And if she's anything like you, it would be an honor and a privilege to name our daughter after your mother. So tell us," said Akka, "what's your mother's name?"

Amos peered down at the ground, sighed, and muttered, "Mema."

"Did you say *Amoeba*?" exclaimed Kumba. "What a beautiful name!"

"A — m e e — b a ," said Akka, carefully sounding out each syllable. "I've never heard that name before. Well, it's official!" he declared. "Our third daughter will be named Amoeba after Amos's mother!"

Amos didn't even try to correct them. He was too discouraged. Once again, he had failed to fire Kumba.

Amos smiled politely and said, "She'd be so touched."

Smiling, the two birds returned to Kumba's nest.

"Amoeba? *Amoeba?*" Amos heard Kumba whisper to Akka. "What kind of a name is *Amoeba?*"

"Must be a family name," said Akka.

"It's a horrible name!" wailed Kumba.

"Shh!" shushed Akka. "Amos will hear you!"

"I'm sorry," said Kumba, "but I hate the name Amoeba!"

"I'm not too wild about it myself," confessed Akka. "But, unfortunately, we're stuck with it now."

Amos spoke up: "You know, Kumba and Akka, it's fine by me if you'd like to change Amoeba's name to some other name."

There was silence from the top of his head. Then Akka called down: "Don't be silly, Amos! We wouldn't think of changing it!"

"Yes, we love the name Amoeba," said Kumba.

Chapter Sixteen
GROWING UP

The next few weeks were the longest days of Amos's life. At first, the baby tick birds did nothing but sleep. But then they did nothing but cheep! Day and night, night and day, all Amos heard was *cheep, cheep, cheep!* It would have been one thing if they were up in a tree somewhere, but they weren't. They were on his head—just inches from his ears.

Fortunately, tick birds grow up fast. Within a few weeks, the baby birds had grown big enough to venture out of their nest. They flitted about, darting from Amos's head to this tree branch, that reed, these bushes.

One afternoon while Amos was sleeping on the riverbank, he was awakened by the sound of sniffling. It came from the top of his head. He lumbered to his feet and waded into the river to have a look at his reflection. He saw Kumba perched beside her nest, dabbing her eyes with a piece of a leaf. Only two of her children were in the nest—Kaza and Amoeba.

"Where's Nyayo?" asked Amos.

"She flew off!" cried Kumba.

"She flew off?" said Amos.

"Yes, she flew off," said Kumba.

"Why did she fly off?" asked Amos.

"Why does any bird leave the nest?"

asked Kumba. "A yearning to see the world. The urge to test your wings. The desire to see how high you can fly. It happens. Akka is searching for her now." Kumba wiped the tears from her eyes. "It's only a matter of time!" she wailed.

"Only a matter of time until what?" asked Amos.

"Until *all* my children leave the nest," replied Kumba. "Then I, too, will have to leave."

"You will?" said Amos in astonishment.

"I'll be so sad, I couldn't possibly stay."

Amos could scarcely believe his ears—or his luck. At last, he had found a way out of his predicament, and he didn't even have to fire Kumba.

Akka searched all day for Nyayo. When

he returned at dusk, he was alone. He looked tired and sad as he flew back to the nest. The moment Kumba saw him, she burst into tears.

While Amos felt sorry for Kumba and Akka, he felt happy for himself. Yes, it was sad that Nyayo had flown off, but it wasn't *that* sad. After all, it wasn't as though she had met with some horrible end. She had simply gone off to be on her own. That's it!

"One gone, two to go," thought Amos.

The next day, Amos awoke to the sound of moaning. He rose and walked into the river and peered at his reflection. Only one baby was in the nest—Amoeba. Akka stood with his wing around Kumba, comforting her.

"Where's Kaza?" asked Amos.

"She's . . . she's . . . " Kumba tried to say when she became too choked up to speak.

"She's flown away," said Akka.

"Oh, I think my heart is breaking!" wailed Kumba.

"Please, dear, don't say that!" said Akka. "Or my heart will break, too!"

While Akka did his best to console Kumba, Amos thought, "That's two gone and one to go."

That night, in anticipation of his soon-to-be freedom, Amos stayed out into the wee hours of the morning celebrating. He celebrated by gorging himself on every plant, reed, leaf, grass, and weed known to hippopotamus. By the time Amos settled down for sleep, the soft reddish glow of dawn was breaking in the east and he had the worst bellyache. The next day, Amos slept past noon. Awakening, he blinked his eyes in the bright sun, yawned, and said, "How are you feeling today, Kumba?"

There was no answer.

"Kumba?" said Amos, raising his head.

Off in the distance, Amos heard a lion roar. In the blistering jungle heat, cicadas buzzed.

"Akka?" said Amos, and held his breath.

Still no sound.

"Amoeba?" said Amos.

Not a peep. Not even a chitter. Could it be? Had it finally happened? Yes, it must have! Amoeba, the last baby, had flown off and Kumba, overcome with grief, had deserted her nest and flown away with Akka.

"Yippeeee, I'm freeeeeeeeeee!" shouted Amos in delight. He hopped to his feet. "I'm free! I'm free! I'm free!" He danced a little jig and sang: "Happy days are here again! Oh, happy days are here again!"

Chapter Seventeen
No, It Can't Be!

Amos could not wait to see Zamu's face when he told him that he had ditched the tick birds. (Amos knew he hadn't really ditched them, but Zamu didn't have to know that.) Amos thought Zamu would be absolutely thrilled to see him tick-bird free.

"This calls for a dramatic entrance!" thought Amos. "A real splash! I'll make a huge, spectacular belly flop!"

Chuckling to himself, Amos turned and faced the river. He crouched down to get a running start.

"On the count of three," he said. "One . . . two . . ."

Suddenly, behind him, Amos heard a fluttering sound. He turned to see what the sound was.

It was Amoeba! She was hovering over his shoulder.

Amos stared in horror. "*No,* it can't be!" he blurted out.

Amos closed his eyes, hoping the bird would vanish. But she was still there when he opened his eyes.

"Cheep! Cheep! Cheep!" she chirped.

"*Aaaaggghhhh!*" cried Amos.

"Cheep! Cheep! Cheep!" said Amoeba.

Amos did what any hippopotamus would have done in a similar situation. He bolted. He galloped through the jungle as fast as a cheetah.

Evidently, Amoeba thought he was playing a game. "Cheep! Cheep! Cheep!" she cried with delight, racing after him.

Amos ran like the blazes through the dense green undergrowth. Amoeba flew like the blazes trying to keep up with him. Amos dashed into the reeds that grew along the river. Arriving at the edge of the water, he stopped and spun about. He was gasping for breath.

Amoeba was nowhere in sight.

"Ha! I lost her!" he cried triumphantly.

But then, off in the distance, Amos heard a faint cheeping sound. The cheeping grew louder and louder. Suddenly, Amoeba flew into view, cheeping her little head off.

Chapter Eighteen
A Curious Thing

Amoeba touched down on a reed. She was as happy as could be.

The same could not be said for Amos. He gritted his teeth and glared at the little bird. "What do you want?" he demanded.

Amos spoke so loudly and so fiercely that Amoeba, frightened, burst into tears.

"Cheep! Cheep! Cheep!" she sobbed.

"I don't know where your parents are, if that's what you want!" said Amos. "Now, please, I beg you, *please* leave me alone!"

Amos turned and walked away. Amoeba

sobbed even harder. As angry as he was, Amos could not bear to hear such sad sobs. Sighing, Amos turned and walked back to Amoeba.

"Hey, c'mon," he said. "Don't cry."

Amoeba did something then that startled Amos. She flew to the top of his head. That's when Amos remembered that he still had a nest attached to his big bald head.

"I'm so used to that darn nest," he muttered, "I forgot it was still up there."

With Amoeba on his head, sobbing, Amos stepped out onto a sandbar. He walked to the end of the sandbar and plopped down. If Kumba and Akka happened to fly by, Amos wanted to make sure that they saw him and, more importantly, Amoeba.

Amoeba sobbed and sobbed. It really began to get on Amos's nerves. To make matters worse, Amos felt a bug creeping up his back. Now that Kumba was gone, who would get rid of his bugs? That was something Amos had not thought of.

The bug made Amos itch. The itch made Amos squirm. Amos hopped up and down, trying to bounce the bug off of his body.

It didn't work. But a curious thing happened. Amoeba stopped crying.

Not only that, she fell asleep!

"Well, what do you know," thought Amos.

Still itching like crazy, Amos sat down to wait. An hour passed. Then two hours. Then three hours. Amos waited and waited—and squirmed and squirmed. He kept hoping that Kumba and Akka would appear. But they didn't. Just as Amos was about to give up hope, he spotted them. The two birds were way down the river, flying in

his direction. They were so far away, they were just two specks in the blue sky.

"*Finally!*" cried Amos, springing to his feet.

As the birds flew closer, they grew bigger and bigger in size. Then they grew *too* big. They weren't tick birds—they were egrets!

As Amos watched the two egrets fly past, he heard a rustling sound from within the reeds. The reeds parted. Out slithered the python.

Amos had forgotten all about the snake. But the python had not forgotten about Amos. As he slid past, he winked at Amos.

It was creepy as anything. Amos shuddered.

Chapter Nineteen
AN UGLY SCENE

Amos watched the python disappear into the jungle. "I wouldn't mind if that snake disappeared out of my life altogether," he thought.

With a sigh, Amos sat down and wondered what he should do next. Gazing down the river, he spotted a black rhinoceros. The huge beast was standing in the shallow part of the river, grazing on some reeds. A tick bird was perched on the rhino's back. The tick bird looked very familiar. In fact, the bird looked just like Kumba's friend Cha.

Taking a closer look, Amos saw that it *was* Cha!

Amos jumped to his feet and hurried over. "Hi there!" he cried.

The black rhino kept right on chewing. Cha, who was nibbling on a bug, ignored him, too.

"Hello, Cha," said Amos, smiling. "Long time no see!"

Cha still did not respond.

"You don't happen to know where I could find Kumba or Akka, do you?" Amos asked.

Cha would not even glance over at him! The black rhino, Amos noticed, was eyeing him in the most unfriendly sort of way. It made Amos very uneasy.

"They're gone," Amos told Cha.

Cha whirled about and scowled at Amos. Venom was in her eyes. "Of course they're gone!" she said. "What do you expect? *You* ruined Kumba's baby shower!"

"Look, I'm sorry about that," Amos apologized.

"I bet you are!"

"I am!" in-
sisted Amos.

The black
rhino spoke
up then. "Hey,
buddy, get lost! My
tick bird is working."

"I just want to ask her a question," said Amos.

The black rhino waved his horn at Amos. "I said buzz off!" he snarled.

Over on the opposite shore, a couple of crocodiles snickered in amusement. They were probably hoping the black rhino would charge and rip Amos to shreds.

Desperate, Amos turned to Cha and pleaded: "Cha, please, I need your help! Where can I find those two tick birds?"

"I told you to scram!" said the black rhino.

"Well, you don't have to be a hothead about it!" Amos heard himself shout at the top of his lungs. Worried that he had made the big rhino even angrier, Amos plunged into the river and quickly paddled away.

Chapter Twenty
HUNGRY

Amos swam until he was safely upstream. He trudged out of the water and plopped down on the grassy riverbank. He could not stop trembling. He gazed at his reflection in the river. He saw that Amoeba lay in her nest, still sound asleep, in a heap of exhaustion.

Amos couldn't believe that she had slept through the entire incident. He peered in disgust at his reflection.

"What a fine specimen of a hippopotamus I am," he grumbled.

Just then, Amoeba awoke. She poked her head up from the nest and blinked sleepily.

"Oh, so *now* you wake up!" said Amos.

Amoeba just stared at him—that is, at his reflection in the water.

"You missed all the fun," continued Amos.

"Cheep!" said Amoeba.

"Sorry, I'm not about to do it again," said Amos.

"Cheep! Cheep!"

"What?" said Amos.

"Cheep! Cheep!"

"I don't understand a word you're saying."

"Cheep! Cheep! Cheep!"

Amos began hopping up and down. This time, though, his hopping did not lull the little bird to sleep. It didn't even quiet her down.

Amos stopped hopping and said, "What is it?"

"Cheep! Cheep! Cheep!"

Peering at his reflection, Amos spotted a bug crawling above his left eye.

"You hungry? Is that your problem?" he asked.

"Cheep! Cheep!"

"There's a bug on my face. It's yours, if you want it. See it? It's above my eye."

Amos scrunched the left side of his face and rolled his pupils toward the bug.

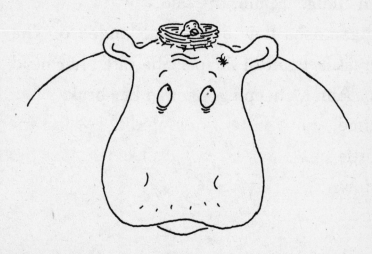

A surprising thing happened. Amoeba smiled. At least, Amos could have sworn she smiled. Amos rolled his eyes again.

This time, Amoeba rolled *her* eyes.

Amos scrunched up his face again.

Amoeba scrunched up her face.

Amos had to chuckle. "Hey, c'mon, you silly bird," he said. "Eat!" He opened his mouth wide as if he was about to swallow a bug.

Amoeba opened her beak wide.

Amos pretended that he was munching on a bug. "Mmm," he said.

Amoeba flew down and landed on the grass in front of Amos. She tilted her head back and, cheeping, opened her beak.

Chapter Twenty-one
RULES

You're not asking what I think you're asking, are you?" asked Amos.

"Cheep! Cheep!" said Amoeba, opening her beak even wider.

"Sorry, I don't feed birds," said Amos.

"Cheep! Cheep!"

"No," said Amos, shaking his head.

"Cheep! Cheep! Cheep!"

Amos, in spite of himself, felt sorry for the little bird. There had been times when he, too, had been hungry. He knew what it was like to have nothing in your stomach.

He knew how awful it made you feel.

"Oh, all right," said Amos. "I'll feed you. But just this once. Got that?"

Amos glanced about to make sure that no animals were watching. Then, quickly, he lifted his front hoof and slapped the bug that was on his face. Holding out his hoof, he presented the squashed bug to Amoeba. The little bird gobbled it up.

Amos chuckled. "I guess you were hungry," he said.

"Cheep!"

"So what am I going to do with you, Amoeba?" asked Amos.

Amoeba smiled.

"Well, until I can think of something, I guess you can stay with me," said Amos. He slapped another bug with his hoof and gave it to Amoeba. "But I do have rules. Rule number one is: *No* getting on my nerves. You got that?"

"Cheep," replied Amoeba.

Amos took that as a yes.

"Rule number two," he said. "*No* disobeying me."

"Cheep! Cheep!"

"And *no* back talk," said Amos. "If there's one thing I can't stand, it's a tick bird that talks back. So . . . *no* getting on nerves, *no* disobeying, and *no* back talk. No, no, and no. Is that perfectly understood?"

"*No!*" replied Amoeba.

"*No?*" cried Amos. "What do you mean n—" He stared at the little bird. "Say that again!" he blurted out excitedly.

"Cheep!"

"I heard you! You talked!"

"Cheep! Cheep!"

"You can cheep all you want," said Amos, "but I know what I heard. You talked! Go on, talk again!"

"*No!*" said Amoeba. "*No! No! No! No!*"

Chapter Twenty-two
TALKING

Once Amoeba learned to talk, there was no stopping her. In the days and weeks that followed, she talked more and more. First, it was just a word here and a word there. Before long, though, she was putting two words together. Then three words. Then whole sentences. Then the next thing Amos knew, she was talking nonstop. She was a little chatterbox, full of observations and questions.

"Look at that cwocodile!" said Amoeba one day while they were at the river. "He

sure is big! Almost as big as you! But
nobody is as big as you. You're the biggest!
How big are you? Will I get big one day, too?"

"Sure," said Amos.

"As big as *you*?" asked Amoeba.

"Well, no, not as big as me."

"Nobody is as big as you, wight?"

"Right," replied Amos.

"What are those things?" asked Amoeba.

"What things?"

"Those globs!"

"What globs?"

"Those globs in the wiver."

"The *what*?" asked Amos.

"The wiver."

"What's a wiver?"

"You know—the wiver."

"You mean *river*?"

"Yes, wiver," said Amoeba.

"It's pronounced *riv-er*," said Amos.

"That's what I said: *wiv-er*."

Amos groaned to himself. He peered at the river to see what Amoeba could possibly be talking about. Big, white, fluffy clouds were reflected in the water.

"You mean those white things?" asked Amos.

"Yes, those white things," said Amoeba.

"Those are clouds," said Amos.

"*Those* are clouds!" cried Amoeba in astonishment. "Why are they white?"

"They're not always white," said Amos. "Sometimes they're dark. That's when you know it's going to rain."

"Wain? What's wain?"

"*Rain,*" said Amos. "You know, that wet stuff that comes down from the sky."

"That's *wain?*" said Amoeba. Then she asked, "What are the clouds doing in the wiver?"

"They're not in the wiver—I mean *river,*" said Amos.

"They're not?"

"No, they're not."

"Where are they?"

"They're in the sky."

"They don't look like they're in the sky."

"Well, they are."

"Are you sure?"

"Yes, I'm sure," said Amos.

Amoeba became alarmed. "Does that mean the sky is in the wiver?" she asked.

"No, the sky is not in the river," replied Amos. "The sky is in the sky." Amos felt a bug land on his neck, near his left ear. It made him itch. "Say, think you could get that bug by my ear?"

But Amoeba didn't. "The sky sure looks like it's in the wiver," she said.

"Well, it's not," said Amos. "That's a reflection you're seeing."

"A *what?*"

"A reflection," said Amos. "A reflection is a . . . " Amos wasn't sure what, exactly, a reflection was. "Never mind," he said.

"So the sky *isn't* in the wiver?" said Amoeba.

"No, it's not," said Amos.

"I sure am glad to hear that," said Amoeba. "I was worried that the sky was in the wiver."

"Well, you don't have to be worried," said Amos. "Now how about getting rid of that bug for me?"

"I want you to feed me," said Amoeba.

"*Oh*, no!" said Amos. "You have to learn to feed yourself."

"I don't like feeding myself," replied Amoeba.

"What do you mean you don't like feeding yourself?" said Amos. "You're a tick bird. Tick birds love to feed themselves bugs."

"Not me," said Amoeba. "I like talking with you."

"Lucky me," groaned Amos.

"You know what I don't understand?" said Amoeba.

"What's that?" sighed Amos.

"If the sky isn't in the wiver, why are the clouds in the wiver?"

Amos shut his eyes and groaned. "*Ugh!*" he cried. "You sound just like your mother!"

Chapter Twenty-three
THE PRETTY HIPPOPOTAMUS

Amos found talking to Amoeba very frustrating. And very exhausting!

It was a hot, steamy afternoon—the kind of day you're glad to be a hippopotamus living along a river. Amos wanted to plunge into the water and cool himself off. But he didn't dare. He was too worried that he might run into Zamu. Amos knew what would happen then. Zamu would give him a hard time about the nest that was still on top of Amos's head.

"I need to find a nice quiet spot up the

river to swim," thought Amos. "Someplace where nobody will see me."

With Amoeba perched on top of his head, Amos trudged up the riverbank. As he was making his way through a thick clump of jungle growth, he spotted, farther up the shore, the prettiest hippopotamus he had ever seen. She was lying in a clearing, sunning herself. Amos opened his eyes wide and stared.

"*Whoa!*" he blurted out. "Look at that hippopotamus!"

"What hippopotamouse?" asked Amoeba.

"*That* hippopotamus!" said Amos. "She's gorgeous!"

"What does goygeous mean?" asked Amoeba.

But Amos was too excited to explain. He lowered his head and made Amoeba hop off.

"Now listen," he said to the little bird. "I need you to stay put. Do you know what staying put means?"

Amoeba shook her head.

"It means you're not going to move from this spot."

"What if I see a twee about to fall on me?" asked Amoeba.

"If you see a tree about to fall on you, you can move," said Amos.

"What if it starts to wain?"

Amos glanced up at the sky. The sky was as blue as could be. "It's not going to rain," he said.

"But what if it does?"

"If it does, you can move under a bush," said Amos.

"What if—"

"Look," said Amos, growing impatient. "If there's an emergency, you can move, okay?"

"Okay," said Amoeba in a small, hurt voice.

Amos realized that perhaps he had spoken too harshly. He felt bad. "I know I sound like a big meanie," he said, "but I really need you to stay put."

"What's a big weenie?" asked Amoeba.

"A big *meanie*," said Amos. "It's someone who's very mean."

"Oh," said Amoeba.

"Okay, I'll be back," said Amos. "Now remember, stay put."

Standing nice and tall, Amos turned and marched toward the pretty hippopotamus.

Chapter Twenty-four
A Joke

Hello there!" announced Amos, smiling.

Amos spoke in a big, bold, booming voice. In fact, his voice was so big and bold and booming that it startled the pretty hippopotamus. It also startled the tick bird that was on her back. The tick bird flew away in fright.

The pretty hippopotamus sat up and peered at Amos.

To Amos's delight, the hippopotamus was even prettier up close. She had a smallish head, the loveliest brown eyes, and just a scant amount of facial whiskers.

"Hello," she said.

Amos wasn't used to speaking to members of the opposite sex. He became very nervous all of a sudden. His heart began to thump.

"I . . . um . . . um . . . I . . . uh . . . I happened to be walking along the wiver—I mean river—when I noticed you lying here," he said. "I . . . uh . . . thought I'd stop by and say hi. *Hi!*"

"Hi," she said.

"My name is—"

The pretty hippopotamus interrupted. "Your name is Amos," she said.

"How did you know?" asked Amos in astonishment.

The pretty hippopotamus lifted her gaze

to the top of Amos's head. "I've heard about you. You're the only hippopotamus with a nest on his head."

In his excitement to meet the pretty hippopotamus, Amos had completely forgotten about the nest.

"Gosh darn that nest!" he muttered under his breath.

Amos gave his head a good hard shake. He shook and he shook. At last, the nest broke free, flying into the air. It landed in the mud, near the edge of the river.

Amos felt he really should explain what a nest was doing on top of his head.

"That nest was just a—"

"A publicity stunt?" interrupted the pretty hippopotamus.

"Well, no, not exactly," said Amos.

"A joke?" she asked.

Amos had intended to tell the pretty hippopotamus that the nest had been a mis-understanding. But, frankly, a joke sounded much better.

"Yes, it was a joke," he said.

"I thought so!" said the pretty hip-popotamus.

"I wanted to see how the other animals on the river would react," said Amos. He gave a hearty chuckle. "You should have seen their faces."

Amos was about to describe some of the faces he had seen when he saw he had lost the pretty hippopotamus's attention. She was gazing at something over by the river.

"Will you look at that!" she cried.

Amos turned to look. He was mortified at what he saw.

Amoeba had not stayed put. She had

flown over to her nest that was lying beside the river. With her beak, she was pulling on a long blade of grass that was attached to the nest. She was tugging at it with all her might.

She was dragging the nest back to Amos!

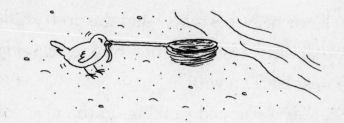

Chapter Twenty-five
SQUIRMING

Well, for heaven's sake," said the pretty hippopotamus. "That little tick bird is bringing the nest back to you!"

Amoeba stopped yanking on the piece of grass. She turned and faced Amos. She looked piping mad. Amos had never seen this side of Amoeba before.

"What did you do to my nest?" she demanded.

The pretty hippopotamus peered at Amos. "This is *her* nest?" she said. "You mean you took a poor little bird's nest and used it for your joke?"

"*No!*" cried Amos. He was horrified she would even think such a thing. "I didn't take her nest! Honest!"

"Then why does she say it's her nest?"

Amos blurted out the first thing that popped into his head. "She's in on the joke, too!" he said. "See, she's my . . . my . . . my tick bird."

As Amos was saying this, he felt a bug dash across his shoulder. It really itched.

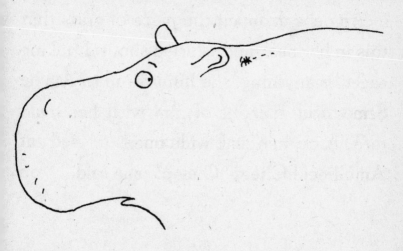

Amos squirmed. He squirmed and he squirmed.

"Is something the matter?" asked the pretty hippopotamus.

"I have a bug on me," explained Amos as he squirmed some more.

"Well, don't just stand there squirming," said the pretty hippopotamus. "Tell your tick bird!"

Before Amos could say a word, the pretty hippopotamus called out: "Oh, little tick bird! Amos has a bug for you!"

Amoeba dropped the piece of grass that was in her beak and whirled about. Looking eager as anything, she hopped up to Amos. She stood in front of him with her head tilted back, her beak wide open.

"Cheep! Cheep! Cheep!" she said.

Chapter Twenty-six

BUT ... BUT ... BUT ...

The pretty hippopotamus stared at Amoeba, then at Amos. She looked totally bewildered. "What is she doing?" she asked.

Amos, of course, knew exactly what Amoeba was doing. She wanted Amos to feed her. But there was no way Amos was going to do that. No way in the world. Not in front of the pretty hippopotamus.

"I'm not sure," said Amos, pretending to be puzzled, too.

Amoeba said, "I want you to feed me!"

The pretty hippopotamus turned to Amos. She had the most horrified expression on her face. "You *feed* your tick bird?"

Amos chuckled. "Of course not!" he said. "What kind of a hippopotamus do you think I am?"

"I'm beginning to wonder," said the pretty hippopotamus.

Amoeba cried out, "You've fed me before!"

"What are you talking about?" asked Amos as if he didn't understand.

"You fed me at the wiver."

"The *what?*" asked the pretty hippopotamus.

"The wiver!" replied Amoeba.

"Oh, you mean that time at the river!"

said Amos. He chuckled again. "You thought I was feeding you? I wasn't feeding you."

"You weren't?" said Amoeba.

"No, I wasn't," said Amos.

"What were you doing?" asked Amoeba.

"Yes, what were you doing?" asked the pretty hippopotamus, eyeing Amos curiously.

Amos smiled and shook his head as if the whole thing was terribly funny. "I happened to lie down on a bug and squished it. It seemed a shame to waste a perfectly good bug. So I gave it to her."

"Sounds to me like you fed your tick bird," said the pretty hippopotamus.

"*See!*" cried Amoeba. "I told you! You did feed me!"

"Gee, you're like her mommy, aren't

you?" said the pretty hippopotamus. A devilish gleam appeared in her brown eyes. Amos did not like this gleam. Not one bit.

"Do you fly, too?" she asked teasingly.

"*No!*" exclaimed Amos.

"Do you lay eggs?"

"Of course not!" replied Amos miserably.

"I've never heard of a hippopotamus

taking care of a tick bird," said the pretty hippopotamus. She began to back away from Amos. "This is getting a little too weird for me. I'm out of here!"

"But . . . but . . . but . . . " stammered Amos.

But the pretty hippopotamus had heard all that she wanted to hear. She spun about and, wading into the river, swam away.

Chapter Twenty-seven
THE EMPTY NEST

Amos glared at Amoeba. "I thought I told you to stay put!" he snarled.

"You said I could move if there was an emoogency," said Amoeba.

"And what, may I ask, was the emergency?"

"My nest!" said Amoeba. "It fell off your head!"

"You call *that* an emergency?" exclaimed Amos. "That was no emergency! I shook it off on purpose!"

Amoeba's eyes widened. She looked startled. "You did?"

"Yes, I did!" replied Amos.

"But it's my home!"

"It was on *my* head!" declared Amos. "I want my head back—the way it was before *you* came along!"

Tears filled Amoeba's eyes. "Why are you being such a big weenie?"

"It's *meanie,* not *weenie!*" bellowed Amos. "You want to know why I'm being such a big meanie? I'll tell you why. I told you to stay put and you didn't!"

"I was just trying to help," explained Amoeba.

"You call that *help?*" cried Amos. "I'll tell you how you can help. *Go!*"

"*Go?*"

"Yes, go! Go and leave me in peace! Is that too much to ask?"

"You want me to go?" asked Amoeba in disbelief.

"Yes, I want you to go. I want you to go away and stay away forever!"

"Forever?"

"Yes, forever and ever!"

Amoeba sniffed. "Okay," she said in a small, hurt voice. "If you really want me to go, I'll go."

But she did not go. She just stood there with the most forlorn expression on her face.

"Good-bye," said Amos.

Amoeba gave Amos a little wave with her wing. Then, bursting into tears, she fluttered off.

"Well, that takes care of that," said Amos.

"I'm a free hippopotamus again!"

It was strange, though. For some reason, freedom did not make Amos feel very happy. In fact, it made him feel just terrible.

"I'm free again. I should be delighted," he thought. "But I'm not!"

Amos's gaze fell upon the nest that was lying on the ground. The grass bowl was tipped over on its side. The nest looked so— so empty. Amos felt lonelier than he had ever felt before.

Much as Amos hated to admit it, he knew why he felt so miserable. It was because of Amoeba. She had not been gone for more than a minute, and already he missed her.

Chapter Twenty-eight
HIM AGAIN!

Amos sprang to his feet. "Amoeba! Amoeba!" he called out. He hurried up the riverbank in the direction that Amoeba had flown off.

There was no response.

Amos made his way through the reeds, glancing all about for Amoeba. Suddenly he stopped.

Just ahead, something stirred in the reeds. Amos peered closer, hoping it was Amoeba.

But it wasn't. It was the python.

"Not *him* again!" groaned Amos.

The snake's beady eyes were focused on an object a few feet away.

Amos lifted his eyes to see what it could be.

He gasped.

Amoeba was perched on a reed, pouting, with her head lowered and her wings crossed.

As Amos opened his mouth to warn the little bird, the python struck. One moment Amoeba was clinging to a reed, the next moment she had vanished without a trace.

"*NOOOOOOOO!*" bellowed Amos at the top of his lungs.

The python, startled, swung around. His cheeks were all puffed out. He had Amoeba inside his mouth.

Amos charged. The python quickly slipped away. He was fast. Amos was faster.

With his teeth, Amos grabbed the snake by the tail. He hurled the reptile, hard, against a large rock.

"*Awwwggh!*" gasped the python.

Amoeba popped out of his mouth. She landed on a clump of grass. She was covered with snake spit and her feathers were all ruffled up. Other than that, though, she seemed fine.

Amos went over and gave Amoeba a little nudge with his nose. She appeared to be in a daze.

"Hey, you okay?" he asked.

In his rush to comfort Amoeba, Amos had taken his eyes off the python. This, as he was about to find out, was a mistake—a *big* mistake.

Chapter Twenty-nine
THE FIGHT

All of a sudden, Amos felt something heavy plop down on his back. The next thing he knew, it was wrapped tightly about his thick waist.

Amos let out a startled *"Hey!"*

The python had slipped up into a tree and taken Amos by surprise. The snake coiled his large, powerful body around Amos's neck, and began to squeeze.

"Aggghhhh!" gasped Amos, unable to breathe.

The python tightened his choke hold.

"I don't like hippopotamuses who make deals and then break them," hissed the python into Amos's ear.

"It was—*agghh!*—a—*agghh!*—misunder—*agghh!*—standing!" Amos tried to explain.

The python, though, was in no mood to listen. He twirled himself around Amos's front legs and pulled. Amos collapsed onto the ground.

Amos and the python rolled across the muddy riverbank. They rolled and they rolled. The more they rolled, the muddier they became. Every time Amos tried to break free, the python strengthened his hold. Clearly, the python intended to finish Amos off.

But Amos had no intention of being finished off. Not with Amoeba standing there watching. This was not how Amos wanted Amoeba to remember him. At least, not if he could help it. Struggling to his feet, Amos made his way over to a tree.

He shouted: "One ... two ... *thhrrreeeeee!*"

With all the strength he had in him,

Amos slammed his body against the trunk of the tree.

"Arrghhhh!" cried the python, loosening his vise-like grip.

Again, Amos pounded the python against the tree. And again and again. Each time he did, the snake loosened his hold a little more.

At last, the python crumpled to the ground and limped off into the jungle.

Amos, breathing hard, called out after him: "And don't you bother us again!"

Chapter Thirty
FULL STEAM AHEAD!

Amoeba, sobbing, rushed to Amos. She wrapped her wings around Amos's front right leg. Or, that is, she tried to—her wingspan was nowhere near wide enough to wrap around Amos's huge leg.

Amos was startled—and touched—that Amoeba was so worried about him. It was then Amos realized that Amoeba was more than just a tick bird to him. She was his friend. He also knew his friend needed cheering up.

"Hop on," he said, lowering his head. "I'll give you a ride."

Amoeba, sniffling, was about to climb aboard when she abruptly turned and flew off into the reeds.

"Hey, where are you going?" called Amos.

A moment later, Amoeba emerged from the reeds. She came hopping out, dragging her nest behind her.

"I should have guessed," said Amos. He leaned down so Amoeba could pull her nest up onto his head.

Once the nest was in place—and Amoeba was in it—Amos waded into the river. He turned to head upstream. But then he changed his mind. Whirling about, he turned to face downstream—in the direction of Zamu and the other hippopotamuses.

An hour ago, Amos would never have dreamed of swimming in that direction. But that was an hour ago. He no longer cared what Zamu thought—or the pretty hippopotamus, or any of the other hippopotamuses, for that matter. They could call him a birdbrain or whatever they pleased, it didn't matter.

He was happy.

Except for one little thing: A bug was crawling on his back, down by his tail. It made him very itchy.

Amos tried to wiggle the bug off his body.

No luck.

Amos gave his body another shake.

Still no luck.

Amos planted his hooves firmly on the sandy river bottom. He got ready to really shake. Suddenly, though, he felt two little feet scamper across his back.

The itching stopped!

"Hey, who was that?" Amos called out.

"That was me!" replied Amoeba.

"That was *you*?" said Amos in surprise.

"Yes, that was me."

"But I thought you didn't like feeding yourself," said Amos.

"I didn't," said Amoeba. "But that was before."

"Before what?" asked Amos.

"Before I caught a bug," said Amoeba. "I had no idea catching bugs was so easy."

"Is it easy?" asked Amos.

"Very easy!" said Amoeba. "You should try it."

"No, thanks," replied Amos. "They're all yours."

"If you say so," said Amoeba. And with that, she raced over and gobbled up another bug that was creeping up Amos's head.

Amos, chuckling, swam out into the deep water. "Full steam ahead!" he cried, and set off down the river.

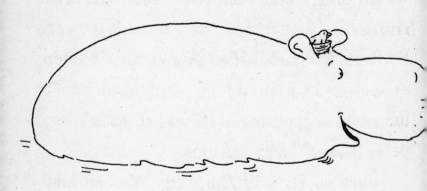

Chapter Thirty-one
REUNITED

It was the end of the day, that wonderful time on the river when the setting sun was about to sink behind the treetops. The river was quieter now, the current slower. Bugs swirled lazily about in the golden evening sunlight. As Amos and Amoeba floated downstream, everything seemed so peaceful.

But then, over on the shore, Amos heard something that wasn't so peaceful. He heard whistling. Loud, shrill whistling. It was the worst whistling Amos had ever heard. Cringing, he glanced in the direction of the sound. He stared in amazement.

There on the riverbank, perched on a dangling vine, were Akka and Kumba. Akka was bobbing up and down as he happily whistled away.

"Well, what do you know!" said Amos.

"I know lots of things," replied Amoeba from atop Amos's head.

"No, I mean, look, Amoeba, it's your mom and dad."

"Where?"

"There," said Amos, nodding toward the two birds.

"Well, what do you know!" said Amoeba.

"Hey, you want to have some fun?" asked Amos.

"Yeah!" said Amoeba eagerly.

"Let's surprise them," whispered Amos. "Hide behind one of my ears."

"Which one?" whispered Amoeba.

"Either one," replied Amos as he began to swim toward shore. "Okay, get ready."

"Get weady for what?" whispered Amoeba from behind Amos's right ear.

"To jump out," said Amos.

"Okay, I'm weady!" said Amoeba.

Amos swam up to Akka and Kumba. "Say, haven't we met before?" he announced.

Amos could not have asked for a better reaction. Akka stopped whistling in mid-note. His eyes bulged out and his bottom beak dropped. Kumba let out a little shriek. They both were perfectly delighted to see Amos again.

"Well, look who we have here!" said Akka.

"It's Amos!" cried Kumba.

"What's with all the whistling?" asked Amos.

"Amos, I am the happiest bird on the river this evening," replied Akka.

"You are?" said Amos.

"I am," said Akka. "I am happy to report that I have finally been offered a job."

"Hey, terrific!" cried Amos.

Akka broke into a big grin. "I start tomorrow."

"Well," said Amos, "I guess it just goes to show that if you put your mind to it, you can accomplish almost anything."

"I can't!" said Kumba.

"You can't?" said Amos.

"No, I can't," she said.

"Can't what?" asked Amos.

"I can't get rid of your bugs anymore!"

"You can't?" said Amos.

"No, I can't!" she said. "I work for a giraffe now."

"That's great!" said Amos.

Kumba looked startled. "It is?"

"Yes, it is," said Amos. "I've found another tick bird. She's a lot like you, Kumba."

The grin on Akka's face vanished. He narrowed his eyes at Amos. "No other bird is like Kumba," Akka informed Amos.

"Oh, but this bird is," insisted Amos.

"Impossible!" said Akka. "Who is it?"

"*Me!*" cried Amoeba, and sprang out from behind Amos's ear. She flew over and landed in front of her parents.

"Amoeba!" cried Kumba and Akka together.

It was the happiest of reunions, with lots of hugs and kisses. At one point, Kumba even flew up and gave Amos a little kiss on his cheek.

Amos blushed. "What's that for?" he asked.

"For taking such good care of Amoeba," said Kumba.

Amos felt his face turn even redder.

"Ah, look, he's blushing!" said Akka with a hearty chuckle. "But then, I, too, would blush if I was a hippopotamus and a pretty bird like Kumba kissed me. We are so much alike,

Amos, it's . . . it's—oh, what's the word I'm thinking of?"

"Spooky?" asked Amos.

Akka gasped. His eyes widened. He looked absolutely incredulous. "That's *exactly* what I was going to say!" he cried. "You're amazing, Amos! You really are!"

Amos just shrugged.